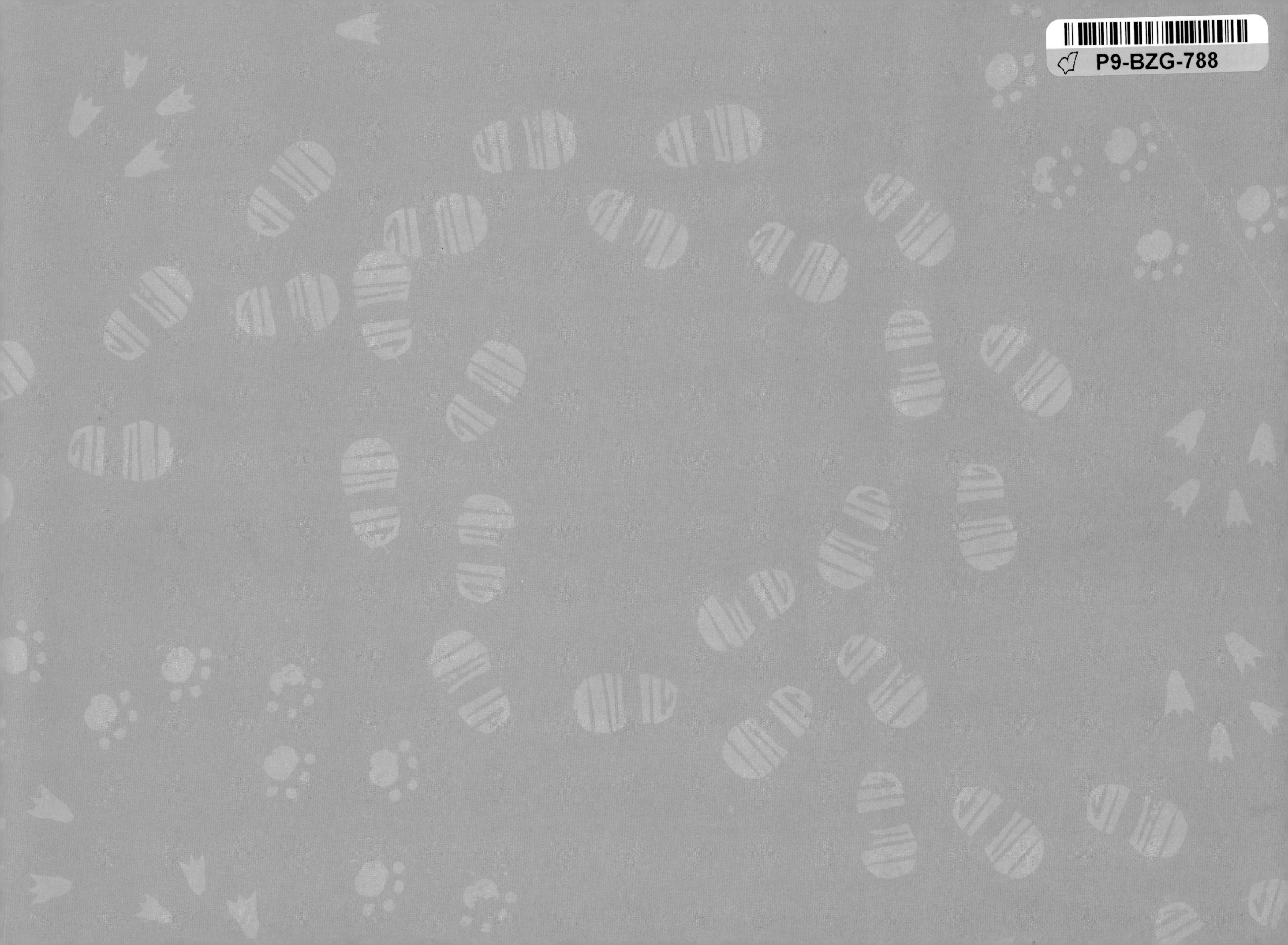

For Elizabeth Wood – M.B.

For my Nain, Grandad and Granna – with love, Cx

Joe
Adele
mara
cassia
Norine

Lively Elizabeth!

WHAT HAPPENS WHEN YOU PUSH

Mara Bergman

Illustrations by
Cassia Thomas

Albert Whitman & Company
Chicago, Illinois

Elizabeth, Elizabeth,
that lively girl Elizabeth,

would kick and stomp and tease and shout,

would point and laugh and run about.

And do some things she shouldn't do,

like hide, then jump out yelling...

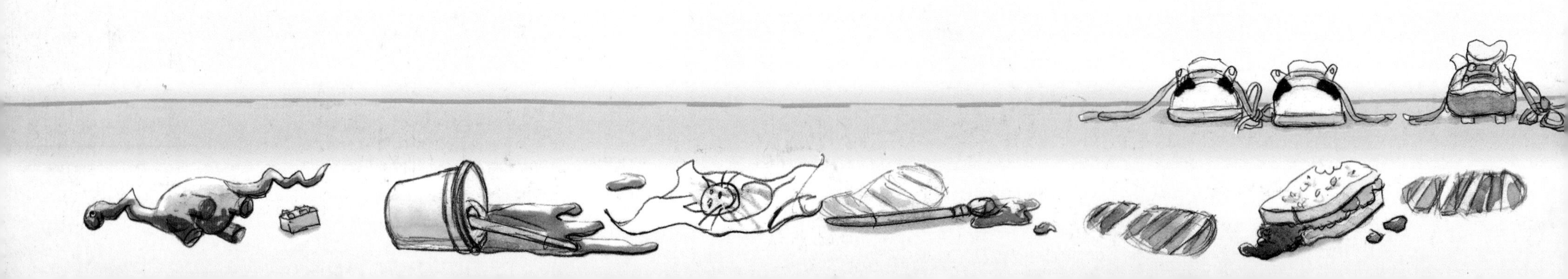

"BOO!"

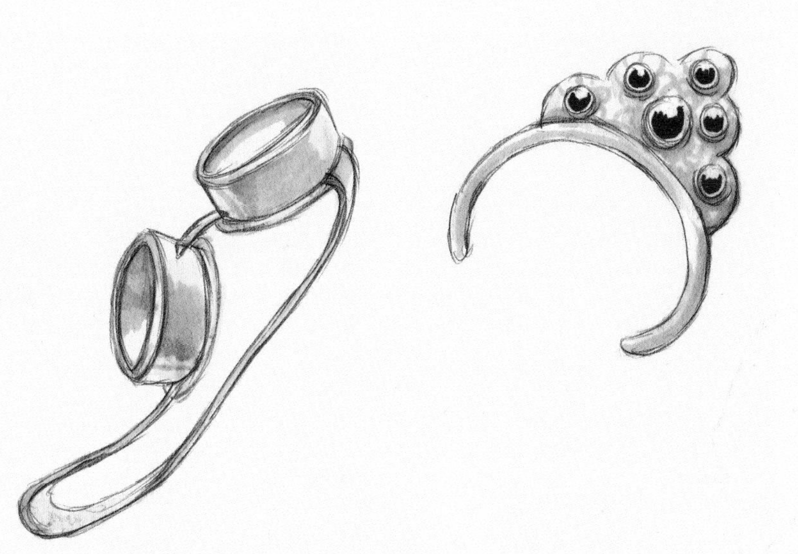

And even though Elizabeth
was lively there was something which
she knew that she should *never* do.

One morning…

SHE PUSHED

JOE FITZHUGH!

And Joe in turn

knocked Ethan Snell,

who tumbled down

on Annabelle,

who bumped Norine

against the wall

so that the books

fell down on...

Saul,

who flew into

Evangeline,

who bounced back like

a trampoline,

so that Adele,

Shaheen, and Dan

went toppling on

Germaine and Anne...

And what a noise that falling made!

CRASH!

BASH!

OUCH!
SMASH!

The classroom went all quiet then.

The first ones up, Germaine and Anne,

glared at Adele, Shaheen, and Dan,

who pointed at Evangeline,

now struggling with a tambourine...

who scowled at Saul, and Norine, too,

who rubbed their knees and found their shoes

as they uncovered Annabelle,

who blamed it on poor Ethan Snell,

who shook his fist at…

Joe Fitzhugh,

whose anger grew and **grew** and **grew!**

Joe looked straight at Elizabeth,
then paused to take a great
big breath

before he yelled…

"WHAT HAVE YOU DONE?

You pushed me and hurt everyone!"

Elizabeth was mighty scared

and said as all the children glared:

"I didn't push you hard at all.

I never meant to make you fall. I am...

very...

VERY...

SORRY!"

Joe thought a bit, then said, "OK.

Now let's all go outside to play!"

The children ran and jumped and skipped,

they danced

and leapt

and hopped

and hipped.

This time nobody pushed or fell.

They laughed and played...

and all was well.

Library of Congress Cataloging-in-Publication Data
is available from the Library of Congress.

ISBN 978-0-8075-4702-1

First published in Great Britain in 2010
by Hodder Children's Books.

Published in 2010 by Albert Whitman & Company.
 Printed in China.

10 9 8 7 6 5 4 3 2 1 WK 14 13 12 11 10 09

For more information about Albert Whitman & Company,
visit our web site at www.albertwhitman.com